THE WHIT□ □ IEES
by Suhay□

Adam and Lily meet in □ □ seaside café in
winter. It's bleak and lonely, and they're both
looking for love. Far out at sea, they can see a
dark shape that moves and shifts. It looks like an
island – but no one else seems to know what it
is. In fact, no one else admits to seeing it.

Adam is a writer who isn't writing anything;
Lily is a waitress who says she is French. But
nothing is what it seems. When they reach the
island it's not black but white. And white cliffs
rise above them. Beneath them, the sea itself, lie
the ghosts of the past.

Suhayl Saadi is an award-winning
Glasgow-based writer. His work has been
published internationally, and also broadcast on
BBC Radio. *The Burning Mirror* (Polygon), a
short story collection, was short-listed for the
Saltire First Book Prize in 2001. He has also
written a radio play, *The Dark Island* (BBC Radio
4), and a novel, *Psychoraag,* (Black and White
Publishing), both app□
www.suhayls

D0258485

THE WHITE CLIFFS

Suhayl Saadi

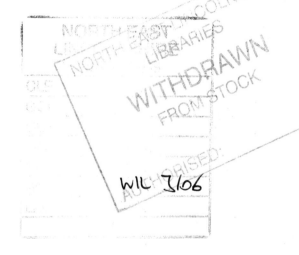

NORTH EAST LINCOLNSHIRE LIBRARIES
NORTH EAST LINCOLNSHIRE LIBRARIES
WITHDRAWN FROM STOCK
AUTHORISED:
WIL 3/06

SANDSTONE vista 3

The Sandstone Vista Series

The White Cliffs by Suhayl Saadi
First published 2004 in Great Britain by Sandstone Press Ltd
PO Box 5725, Dingwall, Ross-shire, IV15 9WJ, Scotland

The publisher acknowledges the financial assistance of the
Literacies Initiative of the Highland Community Learning
Strategy Partnership.

Copyright © 2004 Suhayl Saadi

The moral right of the author has been asserted in accordance
with the Copyright, Designs and Patents Act 1988.

ISBN 0-9546333-1-8

The Sandstone Vista Series of novellas has
been written and skilfully edited
for the enjoyment of readers with differing levels
of reading skills, from the emergent to the accomplished.

Designed and typeset by Edward Garden Graphic Design,
Dingwall, Ross-shire, Scotland.

Printed and bound by Dingwall Printers Ltd,
Dingwall, Ross-shire, Scotland.

SANDSTONEPRESS
SCOTTISH LITERARY PUBLISHING HOUSE

www.sandstonepress.com

To Ellen Estella Mackrill (1902–2002)

THE BEGINNING

When we have no memory, then our lives are built on lies. But sometimes, we lie because we remember. In order to lie safely and well, we read books. If we wish to become kings of tales, then we write books. The biggest tale in this life is love. And perhaps this is why, many years after the event, I decided to put pen to paper and tell this odd story of that winter in Eastbourne. But my memory fails me and so it is up to you, the readers, to decide how much is true. I leave it in your hands.

2

CHAPTER ONE

The first time I saw Lily, she was leaning against the frame of the café door. She was gazing far out to sea, to where the big, black rock sometimes became visible through the mist. We were on the enclosed terrace of a tearoom that sat close to the edge of the chalk cliff. It was a place where you could sit for hours and watch the day go by. To the front of the café was a small, rough garden surrounded by a rickety fence. Beyond that, was an old, whitewashed wall, and beyond that, the ground dipped sharply, eighty or ninety feet, down into the sea. Because roof and walls were mainly glass, it seemed as though the sky and the light were all around me. It was as though already I had left the land. It was as if I was in a boat, floating on the waves of the English Channel.

At first, I didn't call her by name. Not even in

my mind. To me, she was just the waitress who served coffee and lunches in the tearoom. She was the waitress who spoke English with a French accent. At least, I assumed it was French. When I think back, it was like catching waves off the sea. All I can say for certain is that it was definitely not British. We were on the South Coast of England. I was there because, like most writers, I was more or less unemployed, and she was there to work, I suppose.

My life had come to a standstill. My books had dried up. I wasn't even interested in being a writer any more. Like every big thing, it was difficult to pin down why I felt like this. Too much life, perhaps. Or too little. It was possible to live like this in London, indeed, it was an advantage. My father had escaped from Poland in the early part of the century. My mother came from the East End of London, though she was not a Cockney. I was born in Whitechapel, in 1929. I was given the name Adam Arnald Slotsky. The details of a life. Entries in a register: birth dates, death dates. Kingdoms, empires and the small, unknown sacrifices. And in the end, all is forgotten and blown away like dust off the top of a stone. Once, I had wanted only to be a writer. Words had made sense of my world. They had been my religion. I had come to Eastbourne, to try and recapture that difficult magic. I had a little money, but it would not last forever. Sooner or later, I would have to return to the big city. Sooner or later, I would have to set my pen to work, or find some other way of earning a living. But that winter's afternoon, in the tearoom, such thoughts brought only pain.

The truth was, I had noticed her right away, that very first time. I had been in Eastbourne just over two and a half weeks. I had got into the habit of going for long walks along the seafront and up into the hills behind the town. It was one of those afternoons with no wind when the sun shines brightly through a misty sky and yet the air bites like ice. And so, in an effort to warm up, I had decided to climb right to the top of the hill. Even in those days, I was unfit. I was almost dead by the time I reached the summit, and boy, was I glad to find The Old Tearooms. It was a silly name. I mean, to be honest, the place was greasy and very basic. Yet it had been built at the end of the nineteenth century, in the reign of Good

Queen Vickie, I suppose. So it wasn't all lies.

The place was full of people, all dressed in thick, winter clothes and rubbing their palms together. Some of them were smoking. And yet I saw her, the moment I stepped through the door. There she was, just next to the door, gazing out of the window at the sea. A moment later, she was striding across the floor of the terrace. Not hurrying. And then she was bending over one of the round tables, pouring tea from an elegant porcelain pot. She was around five foot-four and had dark brown hair, bound up in a bun. In those days it did not look old fashioned. As she poured, the tea gave off a long line of steam. Then I noticed that all the big, plate-glass windows were covered in a thin film of white steam. Some gentle, classical music danced from the big wooden record player in the far corner. I felt warm. I moved towards the nearest table and slipped off my overcoat. Using my glove, I made a tiny porthole in the window. The mist had cleared a bit, andI marvelled at the sheer size of the ocean. I followed the waves as they rose and swelled and then crashed against the rocks at the foot of the cliff. Hovering on the horizon was the dark triangle she had been watching earlier. I had not noticed it before that afternoon. It felt so peaceful here, the distant sound of the water mixing with the elegance of the violin music, that I could have sat there for hours. An English Sunday afternoon in winter. I was taken quite by surprise when she appeared at my side.

She said nothing, but traced circles with the point of her pencil an inch above her waitress's pad. Feeling awkward, I picked up the menu and scanned down the items. I ordered a mug of white coffee and a cheese-and-tomato sandwich. She was wearing a perfume which I did not recognize. It was sweet and heady, like the first burst of pollen in spring. She frowned. Her eyes were dark brown and would have been black, if the sunlight hadn't been streaming into her face. People make too much of eyes. See, mouths are much more interesting. We read through our mouths. Without a tongue or lips, sentences turn into shapeless dreams. Lips quiver with fear, with pleasure or in the moment before death. Mouths sing and spit and kiss. When they meet again after a long time apart, lovers close their eyes and open their lips. She set the line of her mouth like a blade across her face. I was being shut out. But being totally ignored by women has become a part of my being. I am like an invisible man. It gives me the power to watch. Perhaps, even, to watch myself.

'Oh,' I said, as she turned away, 'and could I have a glass of water, please.'

She paused, but did not turn round. She nodded, ever so slightly, and then moved on. She walked with a slight stoop. It was not something that just anyone would have noticed, but as I have said, I am not just anyone.

'And no ice!' I called out, just before she rounded the corner. This time, she did not stop, but I knew that through the dream music, she had heard.

The place was full by the time my food arrived. It was a Sunday, and everyone was out for the view: Grandmothers with noisy children; lovers whose fingertips touched across the cream-coloured formica; lonely war widows, dreaming of Latin lovers; retired MI5 officers who'd been born with moustaches. The officers tended to glance over their shoulders at the unruly children.

London drowned people, but here, in the place

where the sea cut the land, the faces glowed like moons. Yet I had always stood apart. The waitress, too. I had known it, the moment I had set eyes on her. It was why I had come here. Curiosity: a seeking out of love.

CHAPTER TWO

I soon found out that the woman in the café was called Lily. She knew my name too. I was a regular at The Old Tearooms now, so we had begun talking to each other when she brought my coffee and sandwich.

At the end of the week, I said to her, 'That dark shape on the horizon appeared the very first day I came into this café. I'd never seen it before.'

I had been watching it rise from the horizon. After the first day it did not move an inch along the sea's far edge. She stretched herself over my table, distracting me. Signs of age had already begun to hover over her skin. She smelled of a mixture of winter sweat and dried flowers. Her fingers were broad, with finely-shaped nails, but her skin was rough. I knew she had been a working woman all her life. A lock of her hair swung loose from her bun, but she didn't seem to notice. The hair was lank and the roots were growing in, silver. Where her hair parted I could see her scalp was dry and dead white.

'I don't know,' she shrugged. 'I haven't noticed it before.'

When she spoke, her lips were a thin line. But I knew she was lying. I knew she had watched the horizon every day since I had come here.

'It doesn't look like a ship. Ships are shaped like ships. They're ship-shaped!'

I fumbled the words, and her small breasts danced with laughter. But then suddenly she went red and stood up straight. Gave me a guarded look. She straightened out her overall, and gathered up her pen-and-pad as if it were her armour.

Then, as if she thought this was stupid, she said, quietly, 'Adam, lots of things appear on the sea and then vanish during the night. They slip away, over the waves, while you're not looking. You're out on a boat, and suddenly, mist appears from nowhere and swallows you up. Then all at once the sun burns through again and it's as though nothing had happened. Across the waves of the sea, the world changes.'

It was the first time she had called me by name. She turned away, but by this time of day, all she could do was wipe tables, clear things away. It was after four o'clock, and I was virtually the only customer left. She pulled the grey dishcloth from her waistband and ran it over the surface of the table next to mine. Then she stopped, and stared at me.

'What are you doing here, Adam?'

I glanced down at my coffee mug. The red circle of its outer rim was chipped. The chip took the shape of a mouth. 'I'm drinking coffee. What do you think?' I smiled, nervously, but she did not return my smile.

'I mean, why are you here, why do you keep coming here?'

I looked her straight in the eye.

'Is there some rule against me coming here every day? If you don't need my custom, I shan't come any more. There are plenty of other tea-rooms and coffee houses in this town. Some of them have very good views. Very good views indeed!'

She glanced over her shoulder, as if she was

worried that her boss might have overheard.

'No, no. There's no need for that. I didn't mean anything by it.' She looked at her feet, then back at me.

'I just was interested to know what brings you to this town. To this place.'

I shrugged. Now it was my turn to avoid her gaze.

'I'm on holiday. Isn't that enough?' I said.

'It would be, except that it's not true.'

I looked up. I was startled. How did she know? Her English was almost perfect, as though she had lived here for years.

'Well, you haven't told me anything about yourself,' I said. 'Are you French?'

The only other customer, an old woman, was sitting right at the other end of the café. She seemed to be staring at the wall, but I could tell she was listening closely to our conversation. She had to listen hard because the classical music was really quite loud.

'I was born in the south of France, between the mountains and the sea,' Lily said. In the late afternoon light, she looked older than before.

'But you have lived here for a while,' I said.

'Am I right?'

She did not reply, but just looked at me. I took a deep breath.

'Listen, if you'd like, we could go for a coffee...'

'Another one?' she asked.

'Another one, and you could tell me your story, and I'll tell you mine.'

I spoke quickly, not waiting for an answer. 'When do you get off?'

She cradled the damp dishcloth as though it was a very expensive hankie, or a posy of winter flowers.

'In half-an-hour.'

'Fine then. There's a place down on the front. Sells great ice-cream and pastries. Italian. It's open till late, even in the winter.'

'I know it,' she broke in.

I held her gaze. The light was fading fast.

'I'll finish this,' I said, picking up my mug, 'and then we'll head off.'

So that began the pattern. Every evening, I would meet her at The Old Tearooms just before sunset. We would stroll together down the deserted hill towards the lights of the promenade.

We had to walk about a mile. Some days, by the time we reached the seafront, the biting wind would have turned our faces the colour of blood. One could not have called this love. But it was something. And all the while, the dark pyramid shifted not one inch along the horizon.

CHAPTER THREE

Eastbourne in mid-winter is an interesting place. There are none of the high season shows that like to pretend the War has never ended. None of the rude signs, or the noisy London pensioners. In winter, the town is swept clean by the sea, and the buildings are frozen white by the wind. From October until Easter, the town seems to come into itself. Theatre companies and orchestras come to visit, and the second-hand bookshops in the back streets do a good trade. All the while, the town remains very English, and yet there is the scent of something more. Lily and I moved through those places, and it did not seem odd that two hundred years ago, English Revolutionaries had held meetings in this very town. Perhaps, their graves even lay here, in the red, Sussex earth. It did not even seem strange that witches might gather in attics and cast spells over the roofs. And all the while, through the cold, clear air, fly the ghosts of tall tales.

Lily lived in a one-bedroom, post-War flat at the end of a street. It was right at the foot of the gentle, green hills that swept up behind the town. From her bedroom window, I could see cattle in the fields. They looked peaceful, but they were being fattened for slaughter. This seemed to me unfair. But Lily had been brought up on a farm and she was used to it. She just shrugged, and went on with her work. I liked that girlish quality, so tender in a woman of her age. Perhaps, this time, I thought, I will learn what real love is. But then I became less sure of my own feelings. You can drive yourself round in circles, thinking like that. Better not to think, at all.

Lily was from the deepest part of her country, from a village in the South West of France. She said everything was sharper there. The sun, the moon, life, death. Sharper, no frills. And honesty was the quality which I most admired in her. No lies, no games. She actually said that, on our first night together. She was going to work at The Old Tearooms until Spring. Beyond that, there would be nothing between us. She would return to France, to her cottage deep in the countryside. Then I would slip like a shadow from her life. I suppose I was hoping for something more. She must be lonely, after all. Surely, that was a good enough reason for her to be with me.

She was not beautiful, though she had stayed slim. Her features were thick set and her reddish skin was blemished. She had corns on her feet, because she wore tight modern shoes. And her ankles were thick. I would find unused cigarette papers lying all over her flat. In the morning, she spent the first ten minutes coughing into the sink. She kept herself clean, but didn't seem to bother much about the flat. Almost all of her crockery had been bought at jumble sales, and many of her cups had thin cracks running down the sides.

Beauty is not the same as being attractive. Beauty is the sun breaking in gold through the trees. Beauty is the death of a deer beneath the paw of a lion. Beauty is the moment when my father tossed dry earth down onto my mother's coffin. To me, that winter, Lily was like a tide going out. A gentle yet strong undertow pulling me in, deeper and deeper. Now, all these years later, it surprises me that I find it hard to grab her, know her. It's hard to describe her in words the way I would describe a character from one of my novels. But that's just it. Lily was not invented. Lily was real.

She had got divorced long ago. She was very bitter about her ex-husband. She would say things like, 'He was so cruel,' or 'I had to escape, even from the places that smelled of him.' She really had almost perfect English. In bed, she would glance around furtively. 'Perhaps he will come after me. Perhaps he will come here.' And that was a cue for me to slip my long arm around her shoulders. I would take her head onto my chest and I would let the back of my skull rest against the wall and let my eyes follow the dance of the shadows up on the ceiling. And it was crazy, but I would find myself imagining a giant stranger up there on the peeling plaster. And before falling asleep, she would pull away, turn her back to me. It was as though she wanted to show me that no man could control her. I learned nothing more, though I guessed from the lines around her mouth, that she had suffered betrayal, or loss.

When she lay sleeping and the moonlight caught the angle of her shoulder, she was like a swan. I fell asleep lying next to her body, her lips still hovering over my skin. It would seem like only a few minutes. Yet my nights were filled with strange dreams. In these dreams, sometimes, I was with a younger version of Lily, and we were holding hands and strolling beneath trees by the banks of a river. In other dreams, I was alone, lying in grass and gazing up at the sky. And I woke up to the smell of burnt wood and the lingering touch on my eyelids of a woman's lips. Shafts of sunlight would be streaming through my window and she would be long gone. The dimple in her pillow would have turned cold. I would find her kneeling on a chair and gazing at the mysterious island. She had a wry wit, and smiles would break in waves across her face. She seemed fragile as glass, yet strong as stone. Still, at times, as on that first afternoon in the tearoom, it seemed that she might vanish in the blink of an eye.

We went for walks through graveyards and up into the hills and along the line of the shore.

They were peaceful places, especially out of season. We read the writing on old grave slabs, the ones no one had visited for long years. We traced our fingers along the names and dates. We scraped away the weeds and lichen and that tight, green moss that clings to the corners of lonely places. We invented lives for all the people who had been buried here. The graveyards made us feel more alive. The time before we had met now seemed like a dream. In the place where nothing moved, we were the only points of change. Perhaps we love because we cannot talk with the dead.

CHAPTER FOUR

In mid-February we decided to hire a boat and head out towards the horizon. All the people we had asked about the shape had peered across the Channel and shrugged. They claimed that they could not see the pyramid at all. We even asked the coastguard.

'It's probably a shadow – just the light on the waves,' he said. 'In which case,' he went on, 'it will be like a mirage in the desert or a rainbow over the hills. The closer you think you are, the further away it will get. You might follow it all the way to France, and still you'd never reach it.'

But Lily wasn't letting him get away with that.

'But if it were a mirage, then surely we would have seen it before now. I mean, I've been in this town for several months.' She nodded towards me and slipped her arm through mine. 'Adam here was going for walks and gazing out to sea for weeks before he noticed it.'

The coastguard rounded on her, hands-on-hips. Behind him, his desk sloped up towards the large window and the sky.

'Well, I can't see anything, and that's with binoculars.'

I broke in. 'We've looked through telescopes, and we've always been able to see it.'

The truth was, when we had looked at the object through the promenade viewfinder, it had been no clearer. Just a larger version of itself. A sharp-edged, dark pyramid, floating like the shadow of a yacht sail on the water. And I couldn't be sure, but recently, I had imagined that it was growing larger.

The coastguard just shrugged. He turned away from us and went back to work. I got angry. I stepped forward and grabbed the binoculars from the desk. I looped my hands around his neck and forced the lenses onto his eyes.

'Look!' I shouted. 'Look, you fool! Now tell me you can't see it!'

Lily was tugging at my coat, my shoulders. He was a big man, and with one sweep of his arm, he threw me to the ground. The binoculars clattered into the corner of the room. He said nothing, but his face was bright red. I could see that once he had been a sailor. He glared at me, yet his eyes seemed blind. His chest rose and fell as though he had just run a hundred yards, and his clenched fists hung at his sides. Lily helped me up, and we got out. I almost fell down the steps. We hurried along the promenade until we were sure we were not being chased. Then, tired, we sat on a rock covered with white graffiti.

I was shocked at myself. I had never done anything like this before. Lily did not tell me off, though, and that made me feel it had been worth it. It made me feel as though we had an understanding. Perhaps we did.

And so we hired a small, white boat, a cabin cruiser. It was odd that a waitress was able to steer a sea-going ship. After all, she had grown up in the middle of the countryside. But Lily told me she had worked her passage from France on a large luxury yacht owned by a millionaire. She'd got in with the Second Mate, and had learned to navigate and steer. Lily had the cleverness of a wandering peasant. You could see it in her stride, the way she moved. She carried herself with a confidence and strength which few city folk like me could manage.

It was a perfect morning, crisp and clear as the inside of a diamond. I sat out on the deck, close to the stern, while up on the bridge, Lily steered the boat. There was hardly any breeze, just the light shifting over the waves. As we picked up speed, my hair began to waft around my face and shoulders. I wore my hair shoulder length. In those days, for a man of my age, this was really very unusual indeed. Lily always said my long hair made me look as if I had come from an earlier time.

'It's one of the things I like about you,' she smiled.

The air felt like ice against my skin. I closed my eyes and let the salty morning light slip over my face. I was alone and yet I felt as if somehow I was a part of everything. The waves, the sky, my lover. Everything.

Someone was shouting, over to my right. I opened my eyes. It was Lily. Across the open sea, her voice sounded like that of a teenage boy. I rose and went up onto the bridge. She had slowed the boat. She had pulled the throttle right back, and now she killed the engine, so that we began to drift. The sun was shining straight into my eyes.

I blinked, and rubbed the back of my hand against my eyelids. I needed to be certain that this was not just a mirage or a rainbow, as the Coastguard had put it. The cruiser was drifting towards rocks. Lily ran to the stern and cast the anchor. It seemed to go down a long, long way, but at last, the boat stilled, and there was just a gentle rocking, from side to side. It felt suddenly chilly. We were in the shade, around fifty feet from the foot of the cliff.

It wasn't exactly a pyramid. It did not have smooth sides the way it looked through the binoculars. It was like a mountain, but it was white, not dark. It rose a hundred feet into the sky, like a white cliff against the sea. The light coming off it was so bright, it was painful. I wondered why I hadn't realised that it was white as we approached it. But I had been sitting close to the stern of the boat, facing back towards the coastline. Lily had steered the vessel straight for the island. It struck me as odd that the cliff had seemed so dark when we had watched it from the shore. I decided this must be because of the odd angles and the great distance. It did not occur to me that things might not be what they seemed.

To our right, along the line of the coast, were the elegant buildings on the promenade. Through the binoculars, they reminded me of a row of capped, well-brushed teeth. The red cliffs that framed the town rose like giant shoulders to the west. I peered, but was quite unable to make out The Old Tearooms. That was where I had first had spotted this giant rock. But then, of course, I thought, this island is five or six miles from the coast, in the middle of nowhere. The tearooms, on the other hand, are just a tiny part of a busy coast-line. The hills were partly covered in forest. At this time of year, the trees were dirty brown, so that it seemed as though someone had tossed an ancient fur coat down on the land. Rising from somewhere in the depths of the forest, a thin line of white smoke hung in the sky. Out at the furthest point of the red rock cliffs, the stone had crumbled, and fallen into the sea. I could see that the older rock beneath was the colour of chalk. Among the boulders stood a wrecked lighthouse.

Its white tower was half submerged, and the glass of its windows and lantern had been smashed. I thought of the coastguard, and I wondered why he had lied. Everyone had lied. The man in the bookshop who had sold us some maps of the area, the fisherman out on the end of the pier, even Lily's boss in the café. No one had admitted to seeing this place. Yet it was right here, in front of their eyes. And it was growing. I put my arm around Lily's waist. Shook my head, slowly.

'What is it?' she asked.

'I don't know.'

'It's been getting bigger,' she said, quietly. 'Every time I looked, each day, it seemed to grow.'

I looked down at her. Her hair was wind blown and in the shadow of the cliff, her skin seemed to have aged. And yet, at that moment, in this strange, cold place, six miles out to sea, I loved her more than I had ever loved anyone.

Lily spotted a beach, and we unhitched the rowing boat. We dragged the little wooden boat up onto the shingle, and we sat down and got our breath back. The tiny stones here were dry, but I could feel the cold seep through my trousers into the backs of my thighs. A flock of seagulls circled around the summit. Their cries seemed very far away. She pulled out a cigarette and lit up. There was almost no breeze. We were no longer opposite the English coast, and from the position of the sun in the sky, I reckoned that the beach was facing west. Out here, there were no distractions. I moved up close and we kissed. She tasted of fag smoke, but from her mouth, it was like the scent of rose water. I kissed her again, and pulled her closer.

'I love you,' I whispered, my eyes closing and her smoke filling my head.

We separated, then kissed again, more deeply this time. Behind us, I was vaguely aware of the cabin cruiser rocking on the waves.

'I love you,' I said again.

She did not reply, but just sighed. I remembered that in all the months we had been together, Lily had never spoken French to me. But then, I had not spoken Polish for twenty years or more. So even this ripple of worry sank and was lost in the calm of the midwinter ocean. The pale blue sky swallowed us. My limbs relaxed, and the blood flowed smoothly through my veins. I felt almost weightless.

It was then, as my eyes opened, that I saw the gap in the cliff wall.

Lily must have noticed the change, because she looked up at my face. I nodded towards the crack. She twisted round, and we got up.

Our shoes made crunching noises as we walked. There was a ten foot wide, seven foot high opening in the face of the rock. I peered into the entrance, but all I could see was darkness. The sharp cries of the seagulls seemed even more jagged here, as they echoed against the cliff.

'What is it?' she asked. Her voice was very faint.

'A cave of some sort.'

She looked at me. Her eyes were wide with excitement. 'A smugglers' cave?' she asked.

I shrugged. 'Probably just a tramp's hideout.'

But then, I thought, unless tramps drove speed-boats, it would be rather unlikely that anyone could be using this place. Anyway, this island had appeared only very recently, or so it seemed. But perhaps it was one of those secret places that were used for experiments. Maybe that was why it was off limits. I felt suddenly afraid. What if there were all kinds of bugs and things, scattered amongst the stones and seaweed? Perhaps Lily and I would be poisoned, or arrested. We might even be locked away in some top-secret jail for the rest of our natural lives. Who knew what kinds of things went on, in this old, old country? Things you never heard about in the news. Trained killers with mysterious pasts. Summoning up my courage, I reached out and took hold of Lily's hand. Together, we entered the cave.

CHAPTER FIVE

We were like children exploring a new world. We had expected the cave to be dark and slippery, but it was not. It was almost light, and dry. Slowly, our confidence began to grow. The ground slipped away so that, gradually, the entrance appeared as just a small circle of light. Yet light was coming in from somewhere, though I could not tell how. As we went down towards what I thought was the sea-floor, the cave grew warmer, so that we were forced to take off our coats and scarves and loop them over our arms. But we still held hands. My palm was damp with her sweat, and she was trembling. I stopped, to get my breath. The air here seemed thinner. I let go of Lily's hand and rested my palms on the fronts of my thighs. Lily ran her hand up and down my back.

'Are you alright?' she whispered.

I nodded. 'One minute, and I'll be fine,' I replied.

I wondered why we were whispering. As I straightened up, I stretched my spine, to try and ease the muscles. I was neither young nor fit. As I stretched, I turned. But when I looked behind me, the entrance had vanished. Panicking, I spun round. Lily grabbed my left arm, just above the elbow. She didn't mean to hurt me, but her nails jabbed into my funny bone. I pulled away, sharply. She backed away towards the cave wall.

'The entrance...' I began.

'I think we must have gone round a bend,' she said calmly. 'I'm sure we did.'

'Well why didn't you say?'

She shrugged. Suddenly, it didn't seem so endearing. Her voice was quiet but steady. 'There's only one way out – the way we came. I mean, it's not as if we could get lost.'

I turned on her. 'How the hell do you know?'

Another shrug. The bloody French. And then it occurred to me. I mean, I knew nothing about her, really. Here we were, two middle-aged people, in this cave in the middle of the English

Channel, sweltering in midwinter. I was here because I loved Lily, wasn't I? We decorate our love with carnations and lilies and deadly red roses. But at bottom, most of the time, love seems to be just the desperate need of every human being to feel a little less alone in the big, dark universe. On those terms, then, I was in love with Lily. I laughed, but the sound of my voice was swallowed up.

'What is it?' she asked, coming over to me again.

I shook my head. 'Nothing. It's just... this.' I swept my arm around, to indicate the cave walls.

She took my hand again, more carefully this time, and looked up into my eyes. This time, I did not close them as we kissed.

Lily made out the sound of running water ahead. We began to walk again, faster. Suddenly, we came to a wall.

'This must be the end,' I said, and I reached out and touched the surface of the rock.

The stone felt warm, and it crumbled as I touched it. I rubbed the white dust between thumb and finger. I made a face. It smelt of rotting eggs. I held out my hand to Lily's nose.

In the flickering light, she seemed ten years younger.

'Sulphur,' she said.

She was good at smells. It came from living in the country. She knew the names of all the flowers and trees. She knew how to light a fire from nothing. She knew how to find shelter, and the ways you could trap small animals or gather fresh rainwater. Some of this, she had shown me, on our long walks in the countryside. I was a hopeless townie, so I had envied the way she could do all these things. Farm girl. It was as if Lily knew how to look after herself. On a desert island, or out in the real world, she would survive.

And now she was doing something else. She was scraping away at the rock, at the join between two rocks. Her fingers brushed at the stone, raising a cloud of dust. It made me shade my eyes and want to cough. She scraped hard, like a badger, faster and faster until I could barely make out what she was doing. Through the clouds of white dust, I could hardly see her. Then, all at once, there was a cracking, scraping sound. I grabbed her and pulled on her shoulders, trying to haul her away from the rock face. But she shoved me off, and I fell against the opposite wall. I was surprised at her strength. Farm girl. She glared at me. The sounds died away. Behind her, the crack in the wall had become a dark opening, about a yard wide. She held her hands to her head. Now her hair will be covered in white dust, I thought.

'I'm sorry,' she said. 'I'm sorry.'

But she must have seen that I was gaping at the opening in the wall. She turned again to face it, and then looked back at me. Limply, I held out my hand.

'Wait,' I entreated her. 'Lily, please wait.'

But it was too late. She had already stepped through, and I was alone.

I had to follow her. I had no choice. I found myself squeezing painfully against the powdery stone. My breathing was shallow, and I tried to control the rising panic behind my ribs. What if I got stuck down here? Lily would be trapped on the other side, and no one would ever find us. I thought of the boat, up on the surface, of the sunlight dancing off its clean, white metal hull. I thought of the bite of the wind and the taste of the salt waves, of the rise and fall of the ocean. But all I felt was my chest. And the pain in the skin of my left palm. I could hardly breathe. The pain got worse, and black dots filled my eyes.

Then at last I was through. I sat on the ground, and rubbed my hand. There were five red scratches in the skin. Lily gazed down at me, her face worried.

'God, Lily,' I said, 'do you never trim your nails? It's not good for a waitress. You might crack the crockery. What will The Old Tearooms say then?'

She relaxed, and smiled broadly.

'Poor chap!' she said, in a fake upper-class English accent that sounded odd and stiff, like Chinese.

I got to my feet. We were in a round chamber, about six yards across and three high. The roof was shaped like a tent. At its peak, it disappeared into darkness. The chamber was bathed in dim light. I couldn't see where it was coming from. I turned right round, once. The sound of rushing water grew louder in my ears. I almost had to shout to be heard.

'Well, here we are! We've made it to the

bottom of the sea!'

But Lily was no longer in a jokey mood, and I stopped turning. Just as well, because I was beginning to feel dizzy. She frowned. She was concentrating. It was like when we made love. That was another reason why lovers closed their eyes.

'Adam – ' she began, but then her words were cut off. The deep bass of the water boomed painfully against my ears. I clamped my hands over the sides of my head.

'What is this place?' I mouthed, knowing that she would unable to hear. Lily did not seem to notice the noise. She was gazing at the walls and roof of the cave. The smell had grown stronger, and reminded me of exploded fireworks. A night scent. My ears had stopped hurting, and carefully, I removed my hands. The noise, too, was fading to a faint rushing sound.

'I dreamed of this place,' she whispered. 'Many years ago, in another land, I dreamed of this place.'

She was looking at me. 'Adam,' she said, and the sound of my name was like a song in my head. 'Adam, my love.'

I moved towards her, and held out my arms. But her arms remained by her sides, and something held me back from touching her.

'I lied,' she said. She was matter of fact. There was no passion in her voice.

'What d'you mean?'

'I've never had a husband. I'm not even from France. I'm from a village further along the coast, in Dorset. I was lonely. That was all.'

My legs suddenly felt weak. It was as though the ground was shifting beneath my feet. The West Country lilt in her voice. I felt weak, but I did not want to sit down, not until I'd sorted this out.

'You're joking,' I said, and laughed, nervously. 'It's a joke, right? One of your weird French jokes, that creep up behind me, one of those.' I sounded pathetic. She was looking at me as though I looked pathetic, too. Then I got angry, though I tried not to show it. But the ground was still shifting.

'You mean, you're not from the south of France? You're not escaping from some cruel ex-husband? This whole thing has been a lie?'

She stepped towards me and held out her hand,

but I did not move.

'Not our love, Adam. I did not lie about that.'

'Love?'

She began to pace about the chamber, but there wasn't much room for that, so she seemed like a caged animal. Her accent was no longer French. And yet it still did not sound like Dorset English. I was no longer sure of anything.

'Look. I'm just a waitress. I'm not sure why I did it, Adam. I wanted to be something else, for once. I pretended to be French, and the owner took me on. It worked. I could be anything I wanted. It was like having another life. A life of my own. That was how it started.'

'Yeah, very funny.'

'But then, the dreams began.'

'Dreams...?'

'Look. How much do we really know about another person? How much do we know about ourselves? To make sense of it all, we make up stories. After a while, we begin to live the stories we tell. Eventually, we come to forget. Even The Old Tearooms is a fake. Everyone's a liar. A double-agent. The knowledge of death sharpens our lies into diamonds. My life was like that –

clear, beautiful and empty. Then you came along. I don't expect you to believe me. But what we've had, these past months, has seemed closer to the truth than anything I've ever known. I mean, I wanted to tell you, so many times, but the more we went on, the more difficult it became. I was so lonely. And it was working. I mean, our love.' She sighed. 'This modern world is a terrible place. There is nothing left to pray to.'

'But you lied to me! I told you the truth.'

'What have you told me, Adam? That you came to this town for the winter. That you're attracted to the sea. I know nothing about you, Adam. You say you're a writer. At least I bothered to make up a story. Would you even have noticed me, if I hadn't?'

She paused. I felt as though she could see right through my clothes, my skin. She could see right down to the marrow in my bones.

'Would you even have remembered?' Her fists were clenched, and hung at the sides of her thighs. She spoke more quietly. 'Do you not remember, Adam, my love?'

'Remember what? What are you talking about.'

She looked me in the eye. 'Did you never get

the feeling that we've met before? That long ago, we were going to be married?' She was almost whispering, and her eyes were wild and black like the sky at midnight. I thought that they had been brown, before. Perhaps she had lied about that, too.

'Don't you remember the heat of the sun, the dust, the rats? Have you forgotten, Adam, our meetings by the river, in the time before the plague came? Even though our bodies may change, our names stay the same. Our souls are like stone.'

'What are you talking about?'

The noise of the water was beginning to build up again. I glanced down. Now that my eyes had become accustomed to the dim light, I could see that it was not the floor of the chamber that was shifting, but the sea. The rock was so thin, I could make out the movements of the currents and, now and again, the long, dark forms of fish. And everywhere, a blue-green glow from the giant sheets of plankton. We were standing on the sea wall. Beyond this point, the ocean was bottomless. The pressure of the water against the stone was creating the bass sound that had almost deafened me before. But it seemed less harsh now. Or perhaps I had just got used to it. I was sure now Lily must be quite mad. Yet she was right about me. I had told her nothing.

'Lily.'

'Yes?'

'Is that really your name?'

She shrugged, but did not answer.

'I have had dreams, too...' I began. Suddenly I was angry, and afraid. 'You're a bloody liar!' I shouted. 'I thought you were real, but you were just a fake.'

But I knew I was the fake.

She stared at me, tears rolling down her cheeks. She no longer seemed ten years younger. Her face was centuries old. And she was weeping, loudly. Sobs racked her body. The noise of the water billowed over us and the light from the bottom of the sea grew brighter and brighter until it blinded us. I could hardly think for the noise and the brightness. Then Lily grabbed my long hair in both hands, hard. She whispered in my ear and her voice was like the sea.

'You don't remember, Adam, my love. Ah, your skin is so soft, your hair, so sleek. You've quite forgotten, haven't you? Every night, I take you back, and yet still you do not remember our love. How did it happen? I thought our love would cross the ages. I thought we would flow down together to the mouth of the sea. But you come here only in your dreams, in the night that lies at the heart of life. And then in the morning, you forget.'

I reached out and grabbed her limp arms, just below the shoulders. I shook her. Her hair flowed back and forth over her shoulders, her shoulders that I had held so tight when we were making love. She was right, I could remember nothing. It was as though I had lived always in the polished, white town by the sea. Yet now, my life seemed like the waves beneath my feet. It felt as though every breath I drew might crack me apart. I felt bewildered and angry. Again I thought of the boat, up there in the world of light. I thought of what it would feel like, to lie on its deck, to feel the polished wood at my back. To gaze at the sky, and the white cliffs. I began to cry. And then... then I remembered everything. Our love had spanned the ages. And we had been separated by death. And I wondered what the point was, and I wondered whether there might be no point at all.

'You led me along,' I cried. 'You brought me here, to this place where there is no air and hardly any light, and where the noise of the sea burns in my brain, and now you tell me the truth! But the truth is too painful. Too painful. Why...?' My voice choked off.

'I didn't mean to lie,' she said, quietly. 'I couldn't help it. I didn't know what I was saying. There are too many thoughts in my head. Too many dreams...'

I broke in. 'Why do we have to dig so deep? Can't we just live for the moment? Is this love that we have today not enough? I would have loved you just the same. Now, I don't know who you are. I don't know who I am.'

I pulled her to me. I felt her breasts, her rib-cage, the bones of her hips and knees, the soft moon of her abdomen, press against my body. The scent in her hair wafted across my face, and I knew that she was real. And then I was crying, though I was no longer sure what that meant, since my breath was just one long moan.

CHAPTER SIX

The Year of Our Lord, 1209
The town of Carcassonne, south-west France

For three weeks, now, it had been hotter than ever. The people of Carcassonne were in despair. The sweltering weather and the burning light carried black disease. First to go, one night, had been the verger's wife. Ink marks, the size of coins, burned onto the white skin of her neck. By the time the glowing eye of the sun began to turn slowly in the sky, plague had taken hold of the town.

There had been no rumours about plague from nearby villages, no warning of disease. Very soon, there was no news at all. The town was cut off from all contact with the outside world. Within days, the streets howled with the sound of bells and the roll of carts carrying the grey forms of mothers, daughters, sons and fathers, each turned within six hours to dust. The priests and gentry had run, but they hadn't got far. A troop of soldiers in shimmering armour had been sent by the Count of Toulouse to kill them all, rich and holy alike, and the waters of the River Aude had flowed redder than the sunset. Plague had dropped with black wings from the sky. It would have its fill of blood and flesh and then it would move on.

The lovers lay on the soft, dry tufts of grass that grew over the stones beside the banks of a stream. The girl did not look into his eyes, but instead, tried to gaze at dreamy things, at blades of grass, mushrooms, tree stumps and dancing insects. Yet she found herself drawn back to the stream. She watched the sunbeams dancing on the flowing water. She placed one palm over the left side of her lover's bare chest, while she ran the fingers of her other hand through his hair. She watched the long strands swirl like waves over her skin. The noise of the forest was all around them. The rustling of small animals, the occasional gust of wind in the high branches, and the tinkling of the stream. Beneath everything was a low hum which was the sound of trees, breathing. She closed her eyes and inhaled. It was less humid here, in this clearing. The river, which flowed from high in the mountains, made the air seem cooler and fresher. And for a moment, it seemed to her that he was still breathing.

As the light began to fall, the song of the forest grew louder. The girl knew what she had to do. From her sack, she removed a short-bladed knife and in a single, careful sweep, she sliced off a lock of hair from her lover's head. She rolled up the sleeves of her dress. Her arms were brown and strong. She took hold of his wrists and pulled his body down to the river's edge. She didn't bother to avoid the black sores all over his skin. Kneeling beside him one last time, she closed her eyes and sang a short prayer, though she was no longer sure what she was praying to. Her tears had dried. Now everything was totally clear, her song flowing like light through stained glass.

'At the mouth of the sea, my love,' she whispered. 'In seven hundred years we will be together. When the land grows green again, in the place where the waves meet the white cliffs. Though it may take forever, we will meet at the mouth of the sea.'

Then she opened her eyes, bent down and kissed his lips. Suddenly, with one powerful movement, she turned him into the water. He rolled, face up. He was gazing at the sky, and the sunlight seemed to turn his eyes into hazel. His hair fanned out around his face and the long, brown strands kissed the skin of his cheeks. Through the clear mountain water, his face glowed as though the plague had never come.

'Farewell, my love,' she whispered. 'Fare thee well.'

As the current caught the ends of his ragged clothes, he began to float towards the centre of the river. Within minutes, she had lost sight of him. The sound of the forest became deafening.

CHAPTER SEVEN

Eastbourne, the south coast of England
mid-March 1966

Spring was coming. No leaves yet, but I could no longer see so much light through the trees. Easter would bring the crowds to Eastbourne. I walked to the train station, picked up my ticket and made my way to the compartment I had reserved. I glanced at my watch. If the train was running on time, I had fifteen minutes. I suffered from travel-sickness. Once the carriages started moving and rolling about, I would have to close my book and look out of the window. I would be able to watch the Sussex countryside as I left it behind. If the other passengers were not female, I would make small talk with them. Soon, the big city would seem normal to me again. I would sink back into the miserable mass of London like a tombstone sinking into the earth. It would be as if I had never left the city.

I reached into my coat pocket and drew out a book, which was a little smaller than my hand. It was very old, and smelt musty. I knew now it must be Lily's book, but there was nothing of her in it. I felt sad and then was angry with myself. I looked inside the cover in case there were names of previous owners. But there were none. I flicked through the pages. It was just a romantic Victorian novel. It was nothing special, and the title and author were nothing special. I cannot even remember their names. Sunbeams were shining onto the seat opposite. The bright light made the green leather look even older. My mind drifted.

Love is the only reality we can know. Inside ourselves, there is no other way. It's no good just gazing into a mirror. We learn about ourselves through loving other people. And perhaps, if we get to know, and feel, the characters in a novel, we might just begin to make sense of our own lives. Yet sometimes, I think there is no more wisdom to be found in books than there is in life.

In the boat, on the return voyage that day, we

had remained silent. I had sat at the stern, gazing up at the darkening island and she had steered, tears streaming across her cheeks and hair blowing wildly about her shoulders. But in my mind, now, on the train home, the picture seemed to change. The ship had a tall sail, and though there was barely a breeze, we moved through the night beneath a frozen glass moon. At last, after forty nights, we reached the mouth of the river.

On that last night in Eastbourne, after we had brought the boat back to shore, she rose on tiptoe and kissed me, softly, on the lips. She hugged me. Her arms were wrapped so tightly around my body, I found it hard to breathe. After a while, she looked up. Her tears had dried. Her eyes gleamed like mirrors. We parted there, on the muddy banks, on the creaking wooden boards of the wharf. As she walked away, I called after her,

'We will keep in touch… Lily?'

But she did not look round once, she did not answer. She just gathered up her things and left. Her figure vanished into the shadows as she climbed the slope leading towards the back streets and the graveyards.

A few days after our trip to the island, I

ventured into the tearooms. But the owner told me politely that Lily had left, quite suddenly. She had taken the wages she was owed and left, with the sun at her back, She did not give him a forwarding address. I do not even know whether Lily was her real name. Yet some days later, in my coat pocket, I had found this dusty old book. At first, I imagined that I must have picked it up from a basket in one of the second-hand bookshops, but later, I wasn't sure. It wasn't the sort of book I would have bought. I had put the book back into my coat pocket. It was only now, on the train, that I thought of looking at it again.

I knew that I might return to Eastbourne when the next winter came on, but I also knew that I would never again climb to the top of the white cliffs. And I would never again go back to the strange island, where the sea smelled of sulphur and the light came down off the stone like shining spears.

As I closed the covers of the old book, I noticed some marks in the soft, pink skin of my left palm. One of them had begun to bleed. I placed the book, face up, on the table and reached into my coat pocket for a hankie. When

I drew my hand out, there was a lock of soft brown hair between my fingers It was fastened with a fine, silver thread. The hairs were long and, smooth, and they smelt of roses. I placed the lock in the spine of the book and wiped the blood off on my trousers. Carefully, I closed the book and placed it on the table. I told myself that the marks on my hand had been made by the brass buckles on my case. I told myself, finally, that it had nothing to do with her nails, pressing on the soft skin as she had said goodbye. But I was glad that the train was heading north, and that I would never again catch even a single glimpse of the sea.

Also in the Vista Series:

THE CHERRY SUNDAE COMPANY
by Isla Dewar

You have to bide your time when you live a life
of crime. You have to wait for the moment.
Tina and me discovered that when we founded
The Cherry Sundae Company. Not that we
thought that what we were doing was really
against the law. We were just balancing
things up a bit.

It seemed to us that there was only so much
money in the world and some people had too
much of it. Others hadn't enough. It was our aim
to sort that out. You could say that we were
vigilantes. Of course it all went horribly wrong.
But then, everything that Tina and me
do always does.

Isla Dewar worked as a journalist before
turning to books. She lives in Fife with her
husband, Bob, a cartoonist and illustrator.
She has two sons.

THE BLUE HEN
by Des Dillon

Greenend was rough – the roughest scheme in Coatbridge. John and me thought it couldn't get any rougher. We were wrong. The closing down of the steelworks meant the end of being in work – but John and his pal don't intend it to be the end of keeping afloat. Keep hens – that's the answer. Or become window cleaners? But it's harder than you'd think to be the only honest guys in a place like Greenend.

Des Dillon is an award winning poet, short story writer, novelist and dramatist for film, television and stage. Born and brought up in Coatbridge, Lanarkshire, he was Writer in Residence in Castlemilk, Glasgow 1998–2000. He was TAPS Writer of The Year 2000, and won an SAC Writers' Award in the same year. On World Book Day 2003 his novel *Me and Ma Gal* was voted the book that best evokes contemporary Scotland. He lives in Galloway.

Moira Forsyth, *Series Editor for the Sandstone Vistas, writes:*

The Sandstone Vista Series of novellas has been developed for readers who are not used to reading full length novels, or for those who simply want to enjoy a 'quick read' which is satisfying and well written.

D025851I